DOMINOES

P9-AGM-156

The Curse of Capistrano

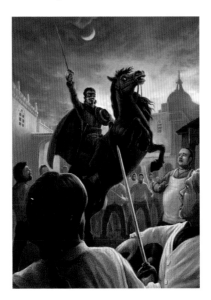

LEVEL TWO   700 HEADWORDS

OXFORD
UNIVERSITY PRESS

Great Clarendon Street, Oxford, OX2 6DP, United Kingdom

Oxford University Press is a department of the University of Oxford.
It furthers the University's objective of excellence in research, scholarship,
and education by publishing worldwide. Oxford is a registered trade
mark of Oxford University Press in the UK and in certain other countries

© Oxford University Press 2011

The moral rights of the author have been asserted

2015

10 9 8 7 6

ISBN: 978 0 19 424924 9   BOOK
ISBN: 978 0 19 424923 2   BOOK AND MULTIROM PACK
MULTIROM NOT AVAILABLE SEPARATELY

Printed in China

This book is printed on paper from certified and well-managed sources

ACKNOWLEDGEMENTS

Illustrations by: Luigi Aimè (All story pages); Mark Draisey p.60 (Paper and quill)

Cover by: Luigi Aimè

*The publisher would like to thank the following for their kind permission to reproduce photographs and
other copyright material*: Alamy Images pp.7 (Garden in Mission Santa Barbara/George Oze),
13 (Santa Barbara Mission/Nik Wheeler), 18 (Potted plant/Richard Wong), 24 (Fort Winfield
Scott, Presidio/Fabian Gonzales), 39 (Vintage wine/Trevor Smith), 47 (Antique pistol/ilian
studio), 54 (Joshua Tree National Park/Michele Falzone); Getty Images p.38 (Latticed window
on stone wall/Felbert+Eickenberg/STOCK4B); iStockphoto p.12 (Door/Mark Wragg).

DOMINOES

Series Editors: Bill Bowler and Sue Parminter

The Curse of Capistrano

Johnston McCulley

Text adaptation by Bill Bowler

Illustrated by Luigi Aimè

Johnston McCulley (1883–1958) was very interested in history. He worked as a reporter and then a public affairs officer in the US army before he began writing fiction. He published *The Curse of Capistrano*, his first Zorro story, in five parts in the *All-Story Weekly* magazine in 1919. In 1920 it was made into a Hollywood movie, *The Mark of Zorro*. McCulley wrote three more Zorro books, and many other stories, before he died in Los Angeles, aged 75.

OXFORD
UNIVERSITY PRESS

BEFORE READING

1 **Here are some of the people in The Curse of Capistrano. Match the sentences with the pictures.**

Sergeant Gonzales   Captain Ramón   Lolita Pulido   Diego Vega

The Governor   Fray Felipe   Carlos Pulido

a He's from a good family, but has little money, and he's Lolita's father.

b He's a soldier who likes drinking, gets angry easily, and is Don Diego's friend.

c She's beautiful, she's from a good family, and she loves Zorro.

d He's from a good family with money, and he wants to marry Lolita.

e He's a good man who works for the church.

f He's a young soldier who is interested in Lolita.

g He works for the King of Spain. He wants to catch Zorro.

2 **Answer these questions about Zorro.**

a Who helps him, do you think?

b Who are his enemies?

c Who does he help

d Who is he under his mask?

Chapter 1 The Sergeant and the Don

In the town of Reina de Los Angeles in south California there was a wild February storm. Inside the **tavern** in the town square, **Sergeant** Gonzales sat by the fire holding an empty **wine** cup. Behind him, four more soldiers sat at a table drinking.

'I'm thirsty!' he called to the **landlord**.

The man hurried over with more wine. Gonzales was famous along the Camino Real – the king's **highway** that crossed the country – because he got angry very easily.

'**Señor** Zorro is on the road again,' the landlord began.

'Why do I always hear his name?' cried Gonzales angrily. 'He rides along the highway wearing a black **mask,** and cutting the letter Z on his enemies' faces with his **sword**. But never when I'm there!'

'They're calling him the **Curse** of Capistrano now!' the landlord said.

tavern an old name for a building by the road where you can eat and drink

sergeant an important soldier

wine a red or white drink that is made from grapes

landlord a man who has a tavern

highway a big, important road across the country

señor (plural **señores**) Mr, in Spanish

mask something that you wear over your face to hide it

sword a long knife for fighting

curse someone or something that makes bad things happen in a place

'He's the curse of *all* our towns, a thief who steals from rich men! The **governor** will pay a lot to the man who kills Zorro. But where to find him? He never comes near the **fort**.'

'But he hides somewhere,' the landlord said. 'One day somebody will find the place.'

'Not if friends are helping him!' cried Gonzales. 'You know, I'd really like him to come in here now.'

Suddenly the door opened, and a man in a wet **cloak** and hat hurried in from the square.

The sergeant's hand went to his sword. But then he saw that it was only his friend **Don** Diego Vega, a rich young man from one of the best families in town.

All along the Camino Real people spoke of these two friends who were so different. Don Diego never wore a sword, never looked at women lovingly, nor drank much. Gonzales always spoke of fighting and women, and drank heavily.

'Ah, Don Diego. We were just talking of Zorro,' Gonzales explained to his friend. 'I want to kill him.'

'Stop there,' said Don Diego in his thin, high voice. 'No talk of killing, please! Zorro fights only those who take from the church or the poor, or hurt **natives**. Why not leave him alone?'

'Because I want the **reward** money!'

'All right then. Just don't talk about it. More wine for my friends, landlord!' Don Diego turned to go.

'Shall I go with you?' asked the sergeant.

'There's no need. I was at home. I wanted some **honey,** so I came for some. Perhaps I'll come back later.'

The landlord gave Don Diego the honey, and the young man paid and left. Then the landlord brought out more wine and everyone drank to Don Diego.

'With his looks and money,' laughed Gonzales. 'I could have

governor a person who looks after a far country for a king or queen

fort a strong building where soldiers live

cloak a big coat with no arms

don an important man from a good Spanish family

native someone who lived in America before white men went there

reward something good that you get for doing something; to give something good to somebody for doing something

honey this is sweet and good to eat; bees make it after visiting flowers

2

any woman in the country and win any fight.'

And the sergeant danced about the room, sword in hand.

'I'd really like to have Señor Zorro before me now!'

Again the door opened, and a man in a wet cloak and hat entered the tavern and locked the door. When he turned, they saw the black mask on his face.

'Zorro!' cried Gonzales. 'What are you doing here?'

'Four days ago you badly hurt a poor native near San Gabriel,' answered Zorro in his strong, deep voice. 'So I've come to teach you a lesson.'

'We'll see about that!' laughed the sergeant, moving nearer, his sword ready in his hand.

Just then, Zorro pulled out a gun from under his cloak. 'Over there!' he cried to the other soldiers and the landlord. 'My gun will stay in my left hand while my sword is in my right. And if any of you move, you die.'

The landlord and the other men hurried into the far corner of the room. Then Zorro turned to Gonzales.

After all the wine, Gonzales moved heavily on his feet. Zorro fought back cleverly, his eyes like cold fire.

Just then somebody knocked on the tavern door.

'Help! Zorro's in here!' shouted Gonzales suddenly.

'You stupid man!' cried Zorro, knocking the sergeant's sword to the floor. Then he hit him across the face with his hand.

'Never hurt a native again,' he cried. Then he climbed out through a window at the back of the tavern – and ran off into the stormy night.

After the landlord unlocked the door, two men from the town ran in, asking, 'What happened?'

'Zorro was here,' explained Sergeant Gonzales. 'He wanted to use his gun on me, but I fought against him, sword to sword. And I nearly won, before he turned and ran.'

Everybody listened to this in silent surprise.

Then Don Diego arrived. 'Gonzales, my friend,' he cried, 'I hear that Zorro came. Where's his dead body?'

The sergeant's face reddened. 'Zorro escaped. I couldn't stop him,' he explained.

'No!' cried his friend. 'After all your talk of killing him!'

'Don't worry. I'll ask **Captain** Ramón to send me after him,' said Gonzales, and he hurried away to the fort.

Don Diego turned to the fire and smiled secretly.

— ♦ —

The next morning – which was sunny and bright – Don Diego, wearing his finest clothes, rode out to the Pulido family's country house. Don Carlos Pulido lived here with his wife and their beautiful daughter Lolita, now eighteen. Don Carlos was an old man from a good family. But he was no friend of the money-hungry Governor, and so was now very poor.

Don Carlos was sitting on the **veranda** when Don Diego rode up. 'Why is Diego here?' he thought. 'Perhaps our luck is changing.' The governor always listened to the Vega family.

'What brings you here?' Don Carlos asked.

'My father says that, at twenty-five, I should marry, so I need a

captain the leader of a group of soldiers

veranda a room with no walls just outside your front door where you can sit out of the sun

4

wife. I've seen your daughter in church – and here I am.'

'Because you'd like to marry Lolita! Right?'

'Yes, Don Carlos. Do you agree to it?'

'I do,' the old man answered. 'I'm very happy for Lolita to marry somebody from the Vega family. But you must ask her yourself.' He called for his wife to come out to the veranda.

'I hope that you can win my daughter's love,' **Doña** Catalina told Don Diego.

'Oh, I don't have time to play the guitar to her,' he replied.

'But, Señor, a young woman likes a man to win her.'

'Then I'll send my **servant** Bernardo with his guitar to play and sing to her tonight.'

'Erm... Do you want to see her now?' Don Carlos asked.

'If I must.'

So Doña Catalina brought Lolita out, and sat at the other end of the veranda. And Don Carlos went inside, leaving the two young people to talk.

doña an important married woman from a good Spanish family

servant a person who works for someone

READING CHECK

Are these sentences true or false? Tick the boxes.

		True	False
a	Gonzales is drinking in the Reina de Los Angeles tavern.	✓	☐
b	Don Diego visits the tavern for some wine.	☐	✓
c	Zorro comes to teach Gonzales a lesson.	✓	☐
d	Zorro and Gonzales fight together with guns.	☐	✓
e	Zorro escapes through the tavern door.	☐	✓
f	Don Diego goes to visit the Pulido family's country house.	✓	☐
g	Don Diego doesn't want to marry Lolita Pulido.	☐	✓
h	Don Carlos is very happy for Don Diego to marry his daughter.	✓	☐

WORD WORK

1 The words don't match the pictures. Correct them.

a mask

.....cloak.....

b honey

....

c cloak

....

d veranda

....

e sword

....

f wine

....

g highway

....

h fort

....

2 Complete the sentences with other new words from Chapter 1 in the correct form.

a ...... *Don* ...... Diego Vega is a rich young man from the town.

b The . *landlord* .... brings wine for the soldiers in the tavern to drink.

c *Sergent* .... Gonzales is one of the more important soldiers at the fort.

d . *Doña* .... Catalina is Lolita's mother.

e .. *Captain* ...... Ramón is the most important soldier at the fort.

f The . *governor* ...... will give money to the man who catches or kills Zorro.

g Gonzales wants to catch Zorro and get the .. *reward* ....

h Some people call Zorro 'the .. *curse* .... of Capistrano'.

i Zorro is angry with Gonzales because he hurt a poor ... *native* ...... near San Gabriel.

GUESS WHAT

What happens in the next chapter? Tick five boxes.

a Don Diego and Lolita talk. ☐

b Lolita agrees to marry Don Diego. ☐

c Zorro meets Lolita in the Pulidos' garden. ☐

d Zorro visits the Pulidos' house. ☐

e Don Carlos sends word to the fort that Zorro is with him. ☐

f Zorro and Don Carlos fight. ☐

g Zorro and Captain Ramón fight. ☐

h Captain Ramón hurts Zorro with his sword. ☐

i Don Diego feels happy when he sees Lolita with Captain Ramón. ☐

Chapter 2 Señorita Lolita

'Will you marry me?' began Don Diego after Lolita sat down.

'Señor,' she cried, 'this is your first visit! You're too quick.'

'**Señorita**,' he replied, 'must I ride over here for weeks before you say "yes"?'

Lolita stood up angrily. 'Don Diego, you must win my **heart**. And if you send your servant to play the guitar to me – yes, I heard that! – I'll drop hot water on him from my window.'

She ran into the house, and her mother followed.

Don Carlos hurried out. 'Women are always difficult at first!' he laughed. 'Next time my daughter will be nicer to you.' He shook hands warmly with Don Diego, who got on his horse and rode slowly away.

At the same time, Doña Catalina was speaking to Lolita inside the house. 'He's rich, from an important family, with a fine face,' she told her daughter.

'But no heart,' cried Lolita. 'I never want to see him again.'

Just then, her father arrived. 'You *will* see him again,' he cried, 'and be more friendly, too.' With that, he left the room.

At **siesta** time, while everyone in the house slept, Lolita went into the back garden.

'If I marry Don Diego, it'll help my father. But I just can't do it!'

She lay down on a seat to rest. But then she felt someone touch her arm. She opened her eyes and sat up. A man stood near her in a dark cloak with a black mask over his face.

'Oh, you're...'

'Zorro, lovely Señorita. I came to your father's house to rest, but then I saw you here, so beautiful! I had to speak to you.'

'I don't know why other men don't feel the same,' said Lolita, her face reddening.

señorita Miss, in Spanish

heart the centre of feeling in someone; this is in your chest and it sends the blood round your body

siesta a time in Spanish-speaking countries when people sleep after lunch

'Do you have no **suitors**?'

'One. But he doesn't like to **court** me.'

'What a stupid man! Courting lights the fire of love.'

'Señor, go now. Perhaps somebody will see you.'

'They'll kill me if they catch me. But I can't leave before I kiss your hand.'

Lolita hurriedly gave him her hand to kiss. Then she ran into the house. Through the window she watched him ride away. 'What a man!' she thought. 'Why can't Don Diego be like *him*?'

— ◆ —

That evening, while the family sat at dinner, Zorro came back.

'Zorro!' cried Don Carlos as the **outlaw** entered the room. Doña Catalina **fainted**.

'I haven't come to steal from you, Señor. You're a good man. I just need food and drink.'

suitor a man who wants a woman to marry him

court (of a man) to try to make a woman love you

outlaw a person who does not do what most people think is right

faint to fall down suddenly because you are ill or afraid

'You'll have it. But can I take my wife to her room?'

'Yes. But your daughter stays here. I want to be sure that you don't run away.'

So Don Carlos carried his wife upstairs. On the way, he sent a servant to the fort to ask the soldiers there for help.

At the same time, Zorro was speaking to Lolita. 'I had to come back to see you.'

'Please never come again.'

Don Carlos arrived back. He did not want Zorro to leave before the soldiers arrived, so he asked him about his adventures. Zorro ate, drank, and talked. Lolita listened interestedly.

After some time Don Carlos got up. 'I'll tell the servants to pack some food for you,' he said.

While he was out of the room, Lolita hurriedly told Zorro, 'My father has sent word to the fort, I'm sure, and the soldiers are coming. Quickly! Go!'

Just then, Don Carlos came back. 'Here's your food for the road,' he said. 'But before you go, one last story, please.'

'No, Señor,' cried Zorro. 'The soldiers from the fort will surely be here any minute.' He pushed over the **candles** on the table and at once the room went dark.

'Until later,' said Zorro softly in Lolita's ear. Then he ran to the back door, and called his horse. Lolita heard the sound of his horse **galloping** away. 'He's escaped!' she thought.

Soon after that, Sergeant Gonzales and his soldiers rode up to the front door. They left at once, hurrying after Zorro. Not long after, Captain Ramón arrived. When he saw Lolita, he decided to wait in the house for the soldiers to come back.

'That Zorro is a **coward**!' the captain said to Don Carlos while he sat with the family.

Suddenly the door of the tall **closet** in the room opened, and

candle it burns and gives light; in the past people used them to see at night

gallop to move fast (of a horse)

coward a person who is often afraid

closet a big piece of furniture where you put things

Zorro came out of it, his sword in his hand.

'Take back those words,' he cried, 'or fight!'

'What?! But we heard you escape!' cried Don Carlos.

'My horse knows when to gallop away without me!' laughed Zorro, 'And when to come back quietly for me, too.'

'You won't escape *me*!' cried Captain Ramón.

The two men fought, but Zorro soon put his sword through his enemy's **shoulder**. Captain Ramón fell to the floor and Zorro put his sword away.

'Don't worry. He'll live!' he laughed. And with one last look at Lolita, he left the house, jumped on his horse, which was waiting, and galloped away.

Soon after this, Don Diego arrived back at the Pulido family's house. He walked in worriedly.

'I heard that Zorro was here,' he explained to Don Carlos. 'So I came to see that you were all alive. But now I understand that my journey wasn't necessary.'

Don Diego was not happy to find Captain Ramón there, nor that Lolita was washing his hurt shoulder. After she finished this job, she went and sat by the fire, and Don Diego went to sit and talk with her there.

Across the room, Captain Ramón quietly told Don Carlos, 'I'd like to marry your daughter, Señor. Does she have any suitors?'

shoulder this is between your neck and your arm

READING CHECK

Put these sentences in order. Number them 1–11.

a Zorro talks with Lolita in the garden. ☐

b Zorro rides away after Lolita kisses his hand. ☐

c Don Diego leaves the Pulidos' house. ☐

d Lolita runs from the veranda to her room. ☑

e Don Carlos sends word to the fort that Zorro is visiting. ☐

f Zorro comes back while the Pulidos are having dinner. ☐

g Captain Ramón arrives at the Pulidos' house. ☐

h Sergeant Gonzales and his men ride after Zorro. ☐

i Zorro and Ramón fight, and Zorro wins and leaves. ☐

j Don Diego sits and talks with Lolita by the fire. ☐

k Zorro comes out a closet where he is hiding. ☐

WORD WORK

1 Find new words from Chapter 2 in the closet.

gallopshoulderfaint
suitoroutlawcourtsiesta
cowardheartcandle

2 Complete these sentences with the words from 1 in the correct form.

a Don Diego must win Señorita Lolita's ....*heart*..... .

b He doesn't want to spend lots of time ...*court*........ her.

c Lolita goes into the garden at ....*siesta*...... time.

d 'Do you have any ...*suitor*......?' Zorro asks Lolita.

e When Zorro enters the room at dinner time, Doña Catalina ....*fainted*..... .

f After Zorro pushes over all the ...*candles*...... on the table, the room is dark.

g Lolita hears the sound of Zorro's horse ..*galloping*..... away.

h Captain Ramón calls Zorro a ...*coward*..... .

i Zorro hurts Ramón's ..*shoulder*....... with his sword.

j The ..*outlaw*........ leaves the Pulidos' house before Don Diego comes back there.
   Zorro

GUESS WHAT

What happens in the next chapter? Tick the boxes.

	Yes	Perhaps	No
a Don Carlos tells the captain that he cannot court Lolita.	☐	☐	☐
b Gonzales arrives with stories of fighting Zorro.	☐	☐	☐
c Lolita agrees to marry Don Diego.	☐	☐	☐
d Don Diego asks the Pulidos to his house in town.	☐	☐	☐
e Don Diego tries to kiss Lolita when she is alone.	☐	☐	☐
f Zorro helps Lolita to escape from Captain Ramón.	☐	☐	☐

Chapter 3 Three suitors

offend to make people angry or unhappy

permission when you agree that somebody can do something

Don Carlos did not want to **offend** either Ramón or Don Diego.

'Señor,' he answered the soldier quietly, 'only this morning I gave Don Diego my **permission** to court Lolita. But if she doesn't agree to marry him...'

'Then I can try!' smiled the captain.

While Lolita sat with Don Diego, she watched Ramón. She knew that he liked her, but she did not like him.

Just then, Gonzales and his men arrived.

'We followed Zorro into the hills,' the sergeant explained. 'Ten other outlaw friends of his came and fought us there, and in the end they all escaped.'

'But the captain fought Señor Zorro here while you were away,' said Don Diego.

'Yes, Sergeant. You were just following Zorro's clever horse which left here without a rider,' went on Ramón. 'I met the criminal himself when he came out of that closet over there and fought against me.'

'No!' cried Gonzales. 'Then we must catch and kill the outlaw. Captain, do I have your permission to take some soldiers and go after him?'

The captain agreed, but Don Diego asked to go too.

14

'It'll be hard work,' said the sergeant.

'Mmm, then perhaps it's better for me to stay in town,' said Don Diego. 'But I'm worried for the Pulidos. So please give me news of where you ride, and of Zorro.'

Soon after this, Ramón and Gonzales left with their men for the fort. Lolita took Don Diego to the door.

'Well, will you marry me?' he asked.

'I'm still thinking about it.'

'Goodnight then, Señorita. I'll visit again soon. Will it offend you if I don't kiss your hand? I'm so tired. Excuse me!'

'Father,' cried Lolita, when the family was alone, 'I *can't* marry Don Diego. There's no life in him.'

'Captain Ramón has also asked to court you,' said her mother.

'He's nearly as bad. I don't like the look in his eyes.'

'You're difficult to please, Lolita,' said her father. 'Don Diego's rich and from a good family. I think that he was **jealous** when he found Captain Ramón here. Make him more jealous, and please try to like him.'

'Yes, Father,' cried Lolita. 'But I don't want to marry him – yet.' And with that, she ran to her room.

In bed, she remembered Zorro kissing her hand. 'What a man! But *why* is he an outlaw?' she said to herself.

— ● —

The next morning Don Diego left his house to find his friend, Sergeant Gonzales, and twenty more soldiers in the town square.

'You're up early!' the sergeant said.

'Yes. I'm leaving for my house in the country,' answered Don Diego. 'But where's Zorro these days?'

'Nowhere near your country house,' laughed his friend. 'We've heard that he's in Pala. We're going after him there.'

'Well, good luck!'

jealous feeling angry or unhappy because someone you like is interested in someone else

Soon after that, Gonzales and his men rode away.

Just before Don Diego left, he wrote a letter and sent his servant Bernardo with it to the Pulidos' house.

— ● —

Don Carlos,

The soldiers have gone after Señor Zorro in Pala. I'm worried for you and your family. I must travel to my country house, but I'd like to invite you, your wife and daughter to stay in my town house while I'm away. You'll be safe there.

Don Diego

— ● —

When the letter arrived, Don Carlos read it to his family. 'What a wonderful plan,' said Doña Catalina. 'What do you say, Lolita?'

'Well, I'd like to visit the town, but is it right? Won't people talk about Don Diego and me?'

'My child, don't worry about that. He won't be there. And we can come home when he arrives back.'

So that afternoon, the Pulido family travelled into town.

Don Diego's house was full of beautiful, expensive things. 'This will all belong to Lolita if she decides to marry him!' thought Doña Catalina.

That evening, Don Carlos took his wife out to visit some friends. Lolita stayed behind, reading a book of love **poetry** that was on Don Diego's table. Strangely, all the books in the house were about love, dangerous adventures, horse-riding, and sword-fighting. 'Perhaps I've made a mistake about him,' she said to herself.

Just then, Captain Ramón knocked at the front door. 'I've

invite to ask someone to come to your home

safe in no danger

poetry short pieces of careful writing; it is often about what you feel

heard that the Pulido family's staying here,' he told the servant who opened it.

'Don Carlos and his wife are out at the moment,' replied the servant. 'Please call tomorrow.'

But Ramón pushed past him and walked into the room where Lolita sat reading.

'Señor!' she cried, standing. 'Why are you here?'

'Last night your father gave me permission to court you. I know that Don Diego wants to marry you too, but surely you can't prefer him to me!'

'Captain, you must leave. I'm alone.'

'Good,' laughed Ramón. 'Then nobody can stop me **kissing** you!' He caught her and pulled her quickly to him. Angrily she **slapped** his face.

'Stop there, Señor,' cried a deep voice behind them.

Ramón turned, and Lolita gave a happy cry when she saw Zorro at the door. 'On your **knees**, man,' said Zorro angrily. 'And say sorry to the señorita.'

With a bad shoulder and no sword to fight with, what could Ramón do? He went on his knees and said sorry, and then Zorro **kicked** him **out** of the house.

'Thank you, Señor,' cried Lolita. Then she suddenly went over to the outlaw and kissed him on the mouth.

'I love you. Leave your criminal life and marry me!'

'Señorita,' Zorro answered, 'I cannot. I love you, but I must go now. Goodnight!'

And, saying that, he climbed out of the window into the dark night.

ACTIVITIES

READING CHECK

Match the sentences with the people.

a Don Carlos — 1 cannot stop Captain Ramón from going into the house.

b Sergeant Gonzales — 2 asks the Pulidos to his house in town.

c Don Diego — 3 tells stories about fighting Zorro in the hills.

d Señorita Lolita — 4 makes Ramón say sorry and leave.

e The servant at the door — 5 tries to kiss Lolita when she is alone.

f Ramón — 6 stays in while Don Carlos and Doña Catalina go out.

g Zorro — 7 says that the captain can court Lolita.

WORD WORK

1 Find nine more words from Chapter 3 in the wordsquare.

P	K	I	C	K	O	U	T	N	J
O	E	S	O	I	L	J	L	E	E
E	M	R	M	N	K	U	R	B	A
T	U	P	M	V	I	S	N	I	L
R	Q	A	R	I	S	S	T	L	O
Y	T	R	W	T	S	L	A	P	U
L	A	A	D	E	C	S	H	F	S
O	F	F	E	N	D	A	I	T	T
O	Z	F	L	S	E	F	R	O	V
U	V	E	K	N	E	E	R	O	N

2 Use the words from 1 in the correct form to complete the sentences.

a Zorro ..kicks out.. Captain Ramón when he finds him in Don Diego's house.

b Does Don Diego feel .jealous. when he finds Captain Ramón with Lolita?

c Don Carlos doesn't want to ..offend.. the captain by saying that the young soldier can't court his daughter Lolita.

d The captain gives Gonzales his .permission. to take some men from the fort and to look for the outlaw Zorro .

e Don Diego ..invites.. the Pulido family to his town house while he is in the country.

18

f Lolita is reading a book of ...Poetry....... when Captain Ramón arrives in the room.

g She ...slapped.....the captain on the face when he pulls her near to him.

h When Zorro arrives, the captain must go on his ....knees...... and say sorry to Lolita.

i Lolita is happy to give Zorro a .....kiss...... on the mouth.

j Lolita feels ....safe...... when Zorro is with her.

GUESS WHAT

Who does what in the next chapter? Complete each sentence with a name.

Captain Ramón

Don Carlos

Don Diego

Señorita Lolita

Sergeant Gonzales

Zorro

a .... writes to the governor about Zorro and the Pulidos.

b .... burns the letter to the governor.

c .... rides out with his men after Zorro.

d .... visits his old friend Fray Felipe.

e .... tells her parents about Captain Ramón's visit.

f .... doesn't think that it's a good plan for Don Diego to visit the captain.

Chapter 4 The letter

Captain Ramón hurried angrily up the hill to the fort.

'Zorro never stays in one place long,' he thought. 'So even if I send my men to Don Diego's house, the outlaw won't be there. I need another plan.'

Once in his office, he sat down and wrote to the governor.

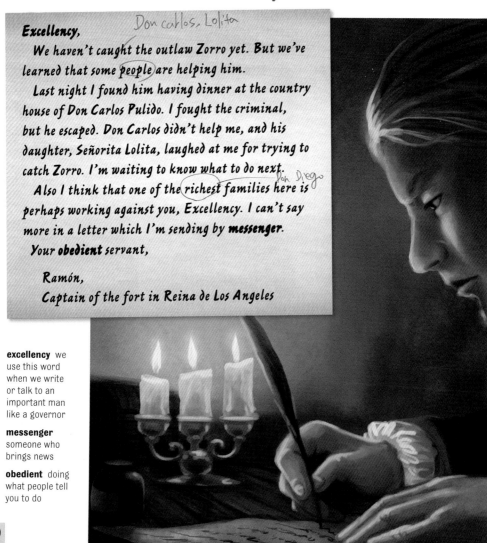

Excellency, *Don carlos, Lolita*

We haven't caught the outlaw Zorro yet. But we've learned that some *people* are helping him.

Last night I found him having dinner at the country house of Don Carlos Pulido. I fought the criminal, but he escaped. Don Carlos didn't help me, and his daughter, Señorita Lolita, laughed at me for trying to catch Zorro. I'm waiting to know what to do next. *Don Diego*

Also I think that one of the *richest* families here is perhaps working against you, Excellency. I can't say more in a letter which I'm sending by **messenger**.

Your **obedient** servant,

Ramón,
Captain of the fort in Reina de Los Angeles

excellency we use this word when we write or talk to an important man like a governor

messenger someone who brings news

obedient doing what people tell you to do

He made a **copy** of the letter. Then he told one of his men to ride with it to the governor's house in San Francisco de Asis. After this, he sat in his office, reading his copy and smiling.

'Soon,' he thought, 'the governor will move against the Pulidos. Perhaps even the Vega family will be in trouble. Lolita won't say "no" when I ask her to marry me again!'

He thought that the 'Curse of Capistrano' was far away by then, but he was wrong.

— ◆ —

Just after he left Don Diego's house, Zorro got on his horse – which was waiting obediently for him – and rode slowly to the fort. He heard a horse galloping away down the highway. 'Perhaps Ramón's **ordering** Gonzales to come back,' he thought.

He knew that most of the soldiers were away in Pala. Quietly he left his horse by a tree, and walked around the fort to Ramón's office window. Inside he saw the captain at his desk reading a letter, and he heard the man talking to himself.

'Lolita will say "yes" to me when her father's in prison,' Ramón laughed loudly.

Quickly Zorro went to the fort door. He came up silently behind the soldier there and hit him on the head with the heavy **handle** of his gun. The man fell and lay still, and Zorro hurried inside to the captain's office, gun in hand.

Ramón looked up when the outlaw came in.

'Don't move or call for help,' said Zorro.

'Why are you here?' asked the captain, his face white.

'I heard you through the window. You were reading a letter aloud. Where is it?'

Ramón gave him the letter and Zorro looked at it quickly. Then the outlaw put it into the **flame** of one of the candles on the desk, and burnt it.

copy when you write something again

order to tell somebody to do something; words that tell somebody to do something

handle the part of a thing that you hold in your hand

flame the bright light that you see when something is on fire

'What a coward to work against Señorita Lolita in this way!' he said. 'Don't try to send another letter like that.'

Just then, they heard the sound of horses and Sergeant Gonzales's voice at the fort door. 'Wait here, men,' cried Gonzales. 'I'll take the news from Pala to the captain. Then we'll ride out again after Zorro – and catch him this time!'

'Sergeant!' shouted Ramón suddenly. 'Quickly! Zorro's here – in my office!'

Gonzales ran into the room. 'Hurry men! We have him!' he shouted. All the soldiers in the fort ran to the captain's office.

Suddenly, with his sword, Zorro knocked the candles from the captain's desk. In the dark, the outlaw caught the captain by the neck and held him. 'I have Captain Ramón,' said Zorro, 'and my gun's at his head. I'm going to walk out of the fort with him. If anyone tries to stop me, your captain will die.'

'Don't do anything stupid, men,' cried Ramón.

So Zorro walked with the captain out of the fort. Then he pushed Ramón to the ground, jumped on his horse, and galloped away down the road to San Gabriel.

Gonzales and his men rode after the outlaw, but they could not find him. Then the sergeant saw the house of the **priest,** Fray Felipe, near the San Gabriel road.

'Zorro always helps the church,' he thought. 'So perhaps Zorro's hiding here.'

He knocked on the door. When the priest opened it, Gonzales and his men hurried inside to look for Zorro, but he found only his old friend Don Diego Vega, who was visiting.

'My dear friend,' said Don Diego, 'I came here for some quiet. With all this talk of Zorro, I'm afraid. I'm going back to my house in town tomorrow.'

After drinking some of the priest's wine with his friend,

priest a man who works for the church

22

Sergeant Gonzales went on his way with his men.

When Lolita told her mother and father about Captain Ramón's visit, and how he tried to kiss her, they were very angry. She also told them how Zorro heard her cry from the street and came to help – but she said nothing about kissing the outlaw.

The next day Don Diego arrived back from the country. Don Carlos and Doña Catalina told him about the captain's visit.

'So, Captain Ramón tried to kiss you,' Don Diego said.

'Yes. I think that he was drinking before he visited me. He smelt of wine. He's an animal! Go to the fort, fight him, and kill him,' Lolita said.

'Must I?'

'If you're a true man – and if you want to marry me – you'll kill this man who's offended me.'

'I'll go and find him,' said Don Diego.

Don Carlos did not think that this was the best plan. But he said nothing, and so Don Diego left for the fort.

READING CHECK

What do they say?

a Don't try to send another letter like that.

b So, Captain Ramón tried to kiss you.

c I came here for some quiet.

d Lolita will say 'yes' to me when her father's in prison.

e If anyone tries to stop me, your captain will die.

f Go to the fort, fight him, and kill him.

g I'll take the news from Pala to the captain.

1 ..d.. Ramón says to himself.

2 ..a.. Zorro says to Ramón.

3 ..g.. Gonzales tells his men.

4 ..e.. Zorro says to the soldiers at the fort.

5 ..c.. Don Diego says to Gonzales.

6 ..b.. Don Diego says to Lolita.

7 ..f.. Lolita says to Don Diego.

WORD WORK

Find the words in the hats to complete the sentences.

a Ramón tells His E.xcellency..., the Governor, that the
Pulidos are helping Zorro.

xeynellecc

b He tells a m.essenger.....to take his letter to the
governor.

negsersem

c Zorro's horse is very o. bedient....... and always does
what he tells it.

ebonited

d Zorro hits a soldier on the head with the h. ahdle........
of his gun.

dahnel

e Zorro finds Ramón reading a c..opy.......... of his letter
to the governor.

ypoc

f He burns it in the f....lame........ of one of the candles
on the desk.

elfma

g Ramón o. rders........ his men not to do anything
stupid.

srodre

h Gonzales thinks that perhaps Zorro is hiding in the
p..hiest........'s house.

setrip

GUESS WHAT

What happens in the next chapter? Tick four boxes.

a Don Diego fights Captain Ramón. ☐

b Captain Ramón says sorry to Don Diego. ☐

c Lolita agrees to marry Don Diego. ☐

d Fray Felipe gets into trouble. ☐

e Zorro fights the men who hurt Fray Felipe. ☐

f Fray Felipe dies in the fight. ☐

g Some young men of the town ride out after Zorro. ☐

h They find the outlaw and bring him to Captain Ramón. ☐

Chapter 5 Justice

At the fort, Don Diego spoke coldly to Captain Ramón.

'You tried to kiss Señorita Lolita at my house last night. That really wasn't very nice.'

'Why is he here with no sword?' thought Ramón.

'Your shoulder was hurt,' his visitor went on. 'You drank some wine before your visit. These things could explain what you did. But I'm courting Señorita Lolita. I'm offended. You must **apologize**.'

'I apologize,' said the captain, hiding a smile. 'But, Don Diego, I went to your house last night looking for Zorro.'

'What?' cried Don Diego.

'The Pulidos are working with him against the governor. Zorro visited your town house when they were there. This shows how friendly they are. Be careful. You don't want to marry a **traitor's** daughter.'

'No,' answered Don Diego.

He went back to his town house where the Pulidos were getting ready to leave for the country the next morning.

'How did things go?' asked Don Carlos.

'Captain Ramón apologized.'

'What are you saying? You mean that you didn't kill him?' cried Lolita. 'Don Diego, I cannot marry a man who won't fight for me!' And she ran out of the room.

'Don't worry,' said Don Carlos. 'When you visit us again, she'll be nicer to you.'

The next morning, after saying goodbye to the Pulidos, Don Diego went to the tavern for a drink. Through the open door, he saw two soldiers riding into town. Between their horses walked a third man, their prisoner.

apologize to say that you are sorry for something

traitor a person who works against his king or country

'What's happening?' asked Don Diego.

'Haven't you heard?' said the landlord. 'They're taking Fray Felipe before the **magistrate**. He sold some bad animal **skins** to a San Gabriel **merchant** who wants **justice**.'

Don Diego hurried to the magistrate's office.

'What's happening to my friend Fray Felipe?' he asked.

'He **cheated** a merchant. Now he must pay,' said the magistrate. The soldiers brought Fray Felipe into the room.

A thin man with a hard, yellow face stood opposite him. 'This priest sold me ten bad animal skins,' he cried.

'Those skins were good,' answered Fray Felipe. 'But if the merchant gives them back, he can have his money back.'

'They smelt bad – so my son burnt them,' said the merchant.

'That's right,' said the boy with him.

'You're doing this because I'm no friend of the governor's,' said Fray Felipe.

'Traitor!' said the magistrate. 'You must pay the money to the merchant in two days. And you've cheated, and spoken against the governor, so you'll have fifteen **lashes** of the **whip**.'

magistrate a person in a small town who says what is right and what is wrong

skin the outside of an animal's body

merchant a person who buys and sells things

justice when someone decides how a person who did wrong must pay for what they did

cheat to get money from someone in a bad way; a person who gets money in a bad way

lash when you hit someone once with a whip

whip a special, long stick for hitting animals; to hit with a special stick

They took the priest outside. Don Diego could not watch, but he heard the noise of the lashes. Fray Felipe himself made no sound. When the soldiers finished, other priests took him back to San Gabriel in a **carriage**.

Don Diego rode after them. When he passed the priests' carriage, he spoke to Fray Felipe.

'My friend, I'm no man of adventure myself, but I hope that Zorro hears of this.'

'Thank you,' said the priest. 'But where are you going?'

'To tell my father about my plan to marry Señorita Pulido, but I'm afraid that she doesn't love me.'

'Did you speak to her of love?' asked the priest.

'No. Why?'

'Try it, and see,' smiled the priest.

At the same time, the merchant and his boy were drinking with the magistrate at the tavern. They laughed about Fray Felipe's fifteen lashes and the money that they would have from him. Later that day, the merchant and his son went back home in their carriage.

But on the road they met Zorro, with a gun in his hand. 'Get down from your carriage!' Zorro shouted, and they did.

'I have no money,' said the merchant. 'A priest cheated me. I took him to Reina de Los Angeles today for justice, but he hasn't paid me yet.'

'I know what happened today,' said Zorro. 'A good priest had fifteen lashes because you told **false** stories about him. You must pay for that.' The outlaw took a whip from under his cloak. He gave the merchant fifteen lashes, and his boy five lashes, before he sent them on their way.

carriage an old kind of car that horses pull

false not true

The magistrate was still in the tavern when Zorro arrived. The landlord was standing by the tavern door with four other men next to him.

'Bring the magistrate here,' the outlaw told them, and they did.

'What's happening?' cried the magistrate when he arrived.

'Today you gave false justice to Fray Felipe. You must pay for that,' said Zorro. Then he turned to the men, 'You must each give the magistrate five lashes with the whip, or I'll shoot you.' They did what he told them.

'If you work against people who are **weak** and poor, this is what happens to you,' cried Zorro.

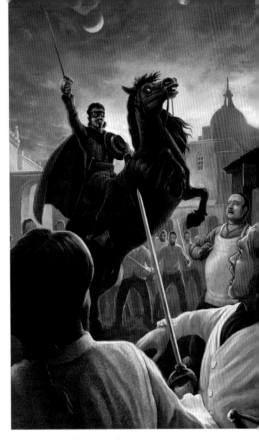

The outlaw told four men to carry the magistrate home, then he turned to the landlord. 'Bring me wine,' he said thirstily.

But when the landlord went into the tavern, he told the rich young men there, 'Zorro's outside. Quick!' They ran out into the square, swords in their hands. There was a big fight. But Zorro was clever, quick, and strong. His horse ran at the young men and stood up on its back legs. His enemies fell back, afraid.

'You're too few for me,' Zorro laughed, and he rode away.

Captain Ramón was terribly angry when he heard the news. And when a number of young men from the town asked to go after Zorro, he agreed.

Thirty of them rode out that night. Some rode to San Gabriel, some to Fray Felipe's house, and some to the house of Don Alejandro Vega, Don Diego's father.

weak not strong

ACTIVITIES

READING CHECK

Choose the right words to complete the sentences.

a Don Diego (talks / fights) with Captain Ramón at the fort.

b A merchant says that (Fray Felipe / Don Diego) sold him some bad animal skins.

c The town magistrate is on the side of the merchant / priest .

d The priest makes a lot of / no noise when they whip him.

e Fray Felipe tells Don Diego to talk to Lolita of money / love .

f On the road home, Zorro whips the magistrale / merchant and his boy.

g Outside the tavern, Zorro orders some young men to whip the landlord / magistrate .

h Thirty soldiers from the fort /young men from the town ride out after Zorro that night.

WORD WORK

Use new words from Chapter 5 in the correct form to complete Don Diego's diary.

Captain Ramón a) apologized to me this morning for offending Lolita. He told me that the Pulidos are b) traitor to the governor and good friends with Zorro, and to be careful about marrying Lolita. Later today, they took my friend Fray Felipe before the town c) magistrate . There a d) merchant with a yellow face told a e) false story about the priest selling him some bad animal f) skins . He explained that Fray Felipe liked g) cheated people out of their money, and that he wanted to have h) justice . The magistrate ordered his officers to give Fray Felipe fifteen i) lashes with the j) whip for his crimes! Poor man! Some other priests took him away in a k) carriage after that. He was very l) weak and could not walk home alone.

30

GUESS WHAT

Who does what in the next chapter? Match the names with what the people do.

a Don Alejandro Vega

1 gives the captain's letter to the governor.

b Zorro

2 tells his son to marry soon or lose the family money.

c Lolita Pulido

3 decides to visit Reina de Los Angeles.

d Ramón's messenger

4 talks to some young men who decide to help him.

e The governor

5 must go to prison with his wife and daughter.

f Don Carlos Pulido

6 tells Don Diego that she cannot marry him.

Chapter 6 Traitors

That evening, Don Diego arrived at his father's house.

'How are you, son?' asked Don Alejandro.

'Tired, father. My journey from town was long.'

Then Don Diego spoke of Zorro's visit to the Pulidos' country house, and of Sergeant Gonzales looking for the outlaw at Fray Felipe's house. Then he went on to tell his father of how they whipped Fray Felipe.

'What cowards – to do this to a priest! But why are you here?'

'I've decided to marry Señorita Lolita Pulido.'

'Fine. She's from a good family.'

'But she's **refused** me, because I didn't court her.'

'Right. So she won't marry you?'

'Don Carlos still hopes so.'

'Then court her! Listen: if you don't marry in three months' time, I'll leave all my money to the church when I die.'

'But Father...'

'I mean it. Why can't you be more like Zorro? He has some life in him at least!'

refuse to say no when somebody asks you to do something

Just then, they heard horses outside, and a knock at the door. A servant opened it, and ten young **gentlemen** walked in with swords and guns at their sides.

'Don Alejandro, we need food and drink,' one of the gentlemen explained. 'We are riding after Zorro.' Then he spoke of the outlaw's visit to the town square and what followed.

'Have you seen the criminal here?' he finished.

'No,' said Don Alejandro.

'Don Diego, did you see him on the highway?'

'I'm thankful that I didn't,' answered the younger Vega.

Then Don Alejandro called for food and wine, and the young gentlemen sat down at the table. Before they started, they put down their swords and guns, and servants moved these to a far corner. Don Alejandro didn't want any trouble.

Soon after this, Don Diego stood up. 'Señores,' he said. 'I'm going to bed. Excuse me.'

'Come back when you've rested,' said one of his friends.

Don Diego went to his room and locked the door.

'What's the matter with him?' Don Alejandro thought.

He sat with his son's friends, who were now drinking and singing loudly.

'I'd really like Señor Zorro to walk in here now,' cried one of them. 'Then we could show him a thing or two.'

'Señores,' came a voice from just inside the front door. Zorro stood there in his cloak and mask, a gun in his hand.

'Give me my sword. I'll stand and fight him,' cried one of the young men sitting at the table.

'After all that wine you won't stand very well,' laughed Zorro.

'Then *I'll* fight you,' said Don Alejandro, getting up angrily. 'I agree with most of what you've done, but you mustn't talk to my **guests** like that.'

gentleman a man from a rich family who does not need to work

guest a person that you invite to your home

33

'I spoke truly, Don Alejandro,' answered Zorro, 'and I refuse to fight you.'

'Then I'll make you,' cried the old man, moving nearer.

'Señores,' said the outlaw, turning to the young men again, 'will you leave this old gentleman to fight in your place?'

'No!' one of them cried. And with that, two of his friends pulled Don Alejandro back to his seat at the table.

'Look at you,' went on Zorro, 'eating, drinking, and forgetting the troubles of those who are poorer and weaker than you. Take your swords in your hands and fight for justice. You're all from good families. You must fight against those who steal in the king's name.'

'Traitor!' cried one young man, jumping up.

'Sit down, or I'll shoot,' went on Zorro. 'Look, I came here to show you how to live better lives. If a group of the best families in the country come together to fight for what's right, the governor will have to agree to change. Here's an adventure. Don't turn your backs on it! Fight against everything that's wrong, and you'll be famous. Or are you afraid?'

'Us? Never!' cried many voices.

'Will you **lead** us?' asked one young man.

'Yes,' answered Zorro.

lead (past **led**) to go in front for others to follow

'But are you a gentleman?' asked another. 'We know neither your face nor your true name.'

'My family's as good as anyone's here,' Zorro answered. 'But for now my face and name must stay secret.'

'Wait. Does Don Alejandro agree with this? We're his guests after all,' said another young man.

'I'm fully behind you,' cried Don Alejandro with fire in his voice. All the young men **cheered**. With the Vegas on their side even the governor would not fight against them.

'What shall we do now?' one of them asked the outlaw.

'Go back to Reina de Los Angeles tomorrow morning. Say that you didn't catch Señor Zorro. Find other young men who think like you. And be ready to fight for justice. I'll send you word when the time comes. Do you agree?'

'We do!'

'Good. And now I must go. Don't try to follow me.' With that, Zorro went quickly out into the dark night, and they heard his horse galloping away.

Then the young men drank to Zorro, justice, and the Vegas. Don Alejandro felt terrible because his only son was asleep through all of this. Just then, Don Diego's door opened, and he came out sleepily. 'Why was everybody cheering?' he asked. 'I couldn't rest with all that noise!'

'Señor Zorro was here,' explained Don Alejandro. 'We have lots to tell you.'

— ◆ —

Next morning, the young men rode back into town with Don Diego. 'Why did Father send me with them?' he said to himself. 'I don't like adventures!'

In the square they met the other young gentlemen who went after Zorro the night before. Some spoke of seeing the outlaw, and the young gentlemen with Don Diego smiled at this.

Then Don Diego went to his house. A little later, in his finest

cheer to shout to show that you are pleased

35

suit and carrying a guitar, he travelled by carriage to visit Señorita Lolita at her father's house.

She sat with him on the veranda, and he told her how they whipped Fray Felipe the day before, and how Zorro whipped the magistrate. She began to like Don Diego better.

But then he said, 'My father will give his money to the church if I don't marry soon. Do you want this to happen?'

'No. But many women would like to marry you, surely.'

'What about you?'

She answered softly, 'You're a gentleman, Señor. So I'll tell you my secret. I refuse to marry a man that I cannot love.'

'So you love another!' said Don Diego.

'Yes, I do.' answered Señorita Lolita.

'But if I stop courting you now, your father will be angry. So I'll go on for a while. It'll stop me going on any more adventures.'

Lolita laughed at these words. Her mother and father heard this, and felt hopeful. Then Don Diego began playing the guitar and singing – badly – to their daughter.

The messenger carrying Captain Ramón's letter had a surprise when he arrived in Santa Barbara. The governor's fine carriage stood outside the fort there. His Excellency was visiting the town, rewarding his friends, and **punishing** his enemies.

The soldier took Ramón's letter to him at once. The governor read it interestedly. 'There's trouble in Reina de Los Angeles,' he told the captain of the Santa Barbara fort. 'I must travel there early tomorrow to stop it.'

The next morning, the same day that Don Diego went courting, the governor and his men arrived in Reina de Los Angeles. He went to the fort and listened to what Captain Ramón could tell him about the Pulidos.

punish to hurt someone because they have done something wrong

'These traitors must go to prison as an example to others,' said the governor. His soldiers left for the Pulidos' house at the same time that Don Diego arrived back in town in his carriage.

Don Carlos's face went white when the soldiers told him, 'Don Carlos Pulido, you're a traitor. You must go to prison at once on the governor's orders.'

But when he learned that Doña Catalina and Lolita had to go with him, he **became** very angry.

'You can't put my wife and daughter with all the town criminals!' he cried. But the soldiers did not listen.

'Why did you refuse Don Diego, daughter?' said Don Carlos after the prison door closed behind them. 'Without him as your husband there's no hope for us.'

'Don't worry, Father,' said Lolita. 'I'm sure that a friend will punish those who have put us here.'

She saw in her heart a man in a black mask and cloak coming to help them.

become (past **became**, **become**) to begin to be

37

READING CHECK

Correct eight more mistakes in the chapter summary.

Don Diego tells his father about his plan to ~~kill~~ *marry* Lolita. Don Alejandro tells his son to do it in

three months' time, or he will leave all his money to the ~~governor~~ *church* when he dies.

A group of rich young men visit the house, looking for ~~Gonzales~~ *Zorro*, but the Vegas have

not seen him. Don Alejandro orders his servants to bring food and ~~guns~~ *wine* to the hungry and

thirsty young men. They sit down at the table – eating, drinking and singing loudly. After

~~Fray Felipe~~ *Don Diego* goes to his room, Zorro arrives. At first, the young men want to fight against

him, but after he ~~sings~~ *talks* to them, they decide to fight on his side and against the governor,

and to help the ~~rich~~ *poor* and weak.

At the same time, Ramón's messenger arrives in Santa Barbara. He gives the ~~priest's~~ *Ramón's*

letter to the governor, who reads it and travels to Reina de Los Angeles. He orders his men

to put Don ~~Alejandro~~ *Carlos* and his family in prison.

WORD WORK

Use the words in the wine bottle to complete the sentences.

a Don Alejandro is an old *gentleman* who is full of life.

b He enjoys inviting lots of *guests* to his house.

c Señorita Lolita *refuse* to marry Don Diego because he doesn't court her.

d The governor decides that he must *punish* Don Carlos.

e Zorro agrees to *lead* the young gentlemen in their fight for justice.

f The young men *cheer* when Don Alejandro says that he is behind them.

g Don Carlos *became* angry when he learns that his wife and daughter are going to prison with him.

becomes
cheer
gentleman

guests
lead
punish
refuses

GUESS WHAT

What happens in the next chapter? Tick the boxes.

	Yes	No
a Don Diego speaks to the governor about the Pulidos.	☐	☐
b The governor decides that the Pulidos are not traitors and can go free.	☐	☐
c The Pulidos escape from prison with the help of Zorro and his men.	☐	☐
d Zorro takes Señorita Lolita to the house of a friend.	☐	☐
e Sergeant Gonzales rides after Zorro.	☐	☐
f Gonzales catches Zorro, and takes him to the governor.	☐	☐
g Lolita kills herself because she does not want to go back to prison.	☐	☐

Chapter 7 Escape

An hour after they put the Pulidos in prison, Don Diego visited the governor up at the fort.

'I'm happy to see you,' said His Excellency. 'In times of trouble it's important to know who your friends are.'

'I'm sorry that I couldn't come sooner, but I was away from home when you arrived. How long will you stay?'

'I'll wait for them to bring Zorro to me, dead or alive. Captain Ramón has ordered Sergeant Gonzales to **return**, and I have twenty soldiers here, too. We'll catch the Curse of Capistrano this time, I'm sure.'

'Let's hope that all ends well,' said Don Diego.

'These are difficult times,' said the governor. 'Only today I had to order the **arrest** of a gentleman, his wife, and daughter. But the country must be safe from the king's enemies.'

'You mean the Pulido family.'

'I do.'

'Can I speak to you about that? I'm courting Don Carlos's daughter, you see.'

'But you're not **engaged to** her? Because I've learned that the Pulidos are helping Zorro. You wouldn't like to marry into a family of traitors.'

'But to put a gentleman's family in prison with **common** criminals, Señor – other gentlemen won't think it right.'

'But if I put them under arrest at home, this outlaw Zorro will **rescue** them. Prison's the only answer.'

'I see,' said Don Diego.

'You're no friend of the king's enemies, I hope.'

'I'm against all the king's real enemies.'

'I'm happy to hear it,' said the governor.

return to come or go back somewhere

arrest when you take a person to prison; to take a person to prison

engaged to going to marry

common not from a good family

rescue to take someone away from something dangerous; when you take someone away from something dangerous

After Don Diego left, the governor told Captain Ramón, 'You once thought that Don Diego was perhaps a traitor, too, but I tell you that he's too weak, too stupid, and too cowardly for that!' They both laughed.

— ◆ —

On his way home, Don Diego met a friend in the town square.

'Has our leader sent word to you?' asked the young gentleman quietly in Don Diego's ear.

'No. Why?'

'The Pulidos are in prison. We think that Señor Zorro will try to rescue them.'

'I hope not,' said Don Diego. 'I'm starting to feel ill just thinking of it. I must go home to bed.'

'I hope that you are better soon,' laughed his friend.

— ◆ —

Later that day, a native spoke to the same young man.

'A gentleman asks you and your friends to meet him at midnight behind the hill near the San Gabriel road. He told me to say that a **fox** is in the **neighbourhood**.'

The young man smiled. 'Zorro' was Spanish for 'fox'. He went to tell his friends.

fox a clever red animal like a dog with a long tail

neighbourhood all the places near your home

Just before twelve that night, a group of young gentlemen from the town rode out to meet their leader. They all wore masks and had guns and swords at their sides.

'Are you all here?' asked Zorro when they arrived.

'Twenty-nine of us are,' came the answer. 'Don Diego's ill in bed and seeing nobody.' They all laughed.

'Right. Now you know why I've called you here. We must rescue the Pulido family from prison. Here's my plan...'

The young men listened carefully.

guard someone who stops prisoners from running away; someone who stops people from going into a building

cell a room where you lock prisoners in a prison

Soon after that, Zorro and his followers rode to the prison and knocked on the door.

'Who's there?' came the **guard**'s voice from inside.

'Zorro. Open the door now, and don't call for help – or you die.'

The door opened, and Zorro and the others hurried in. They quickly unlocked the door to the prison **cell**. The Pulidos were sitting together inside, far from the common prisoners.

'Señor Zorro!' cried Don Carlos. 'What are you doing here?'

'I've come to rescue you. Let's go.'

'I'm staying,' answered the old man. 'I'm ready to take what comes to me. They say that I gave you a place to hide. What will they say if you help me to escape?'

'Señor, this is no place for you or your family to stay the night. Gentlemen!' he called.

At once two of his followers took Don Carlos from the cell, two others took Doña Catalina with them, and Zorro himself held Lolita's hand and led her from the place.

'You'll be safe with me,' he said.

'I know,' she replied.

But while they were leaving the building, two of Captain Ramón's men arrived, bringing a thief to the prison. They knew from the masks on the faces of Zorro's followers that something was wrong, and they began shooting. Sergeant Gonzales and others hurried from the tavern at the noise. Just then, the prison guard shouted, 'Zorro's rescuing the Pulidos!'

'Quick! To the prison!' cried Gonzales. 'There's a reward for the man who catches Zorro!'

The soldiers at the fort heard the noise, too, and hurried down to the town at once.

By then, Zorro was on his horse with Señorita Lolita sitting in front of him. Don Carlos was on another horse, still shouting that he didn't want rescuing, and Doña Catalina was on a third horse, with one of Zorro's followers behind her. She fainted into this young man's arms.

The rescuers quickly crossed the town square and rode to the highway. There they **divided** into three, following Zorro's plan. Some took Doña Catalina to the Pulidos' country house. Others took Don Carlos along the road to Pala, to hide the old man in

divide to make one large group into a number of smaller groups

the **hut** of a friendly native there. Zorro rode with Lolita to Fray Felipe's house where she would be safe.

The outlaw smiled while he galloped, with Lolita in his arms, along the San Gabriel road. 'At least the soldiers following us must divide into three,' he thought.

After a long, hard ride, Zorro's horse arrived at Fray Felipe's house. The outlaw jumped to the ground and helped the young señorita down. He knocked loudly on the priest's door, and when it opened he took Lolita inside. A minute later Fray Felipe was saying goodbye to the outlaw on the veranda.

'I'll send word soon,' said Zorro.

'Good,' said the priest. He went in, and locked the door.

Zorro hurried across to his horse. Just then, a group of soldiers rode over the hill. They saw the outlaw in the silver light of the moon. 'There he is, men,' cried Sergeant Gonzales. 'After him! The governor will punish us if we don't take him now.'

Zorro jumped on his horse's back, and rode away. He heard soldiers' horses following him, and the men's angry cries. But with only one rider to carry now, his horse moved faster than before, and he started to leave these noises behind.

When the moon went behind a cloud, Zorro left the highway and rode in the dark to a native's hut just by the road.

'They're after me,' he called to the native, who quickly took both the outlaw and his horse inside his hut. Zorro hid there silently while the soldiers galloped nearer along the highway.

'At least Señorita Lolita's safe,' he said to himself.

Back at Fray Felipe's house, Sergeant Gonzales and the other half of his men got off their horses and walked to the house. The sergeant knocked at the door.

hut a little house   'What do you want?' asked the priest when he opened it.

'We're looking for something that Señor Zorro left behind,' said Gonzales, pushing past. 'His horse was slower than usual. He brought a young woman here for you to hide, didn't he?'

'I don't know what you mean,' the priest answered, smiling.

Gonzales knew that Lolita was there somewhere. He sent his men to look in the different rooms of the house and the buildings around it, but he himself stayed with Fray Felipe.

Suddenly he looked at a tall **pile** of animal skins in the corner of the room. 'What's behind that?' he said.

Señorita Lolita came out from behind the skins with a long skinner's knife in her hand.

'I'm leaving. Don't try to stop me,' she said. 'If you do, I'll kill myself. The governor won't like that.'

'True,' thought Gonzales. 'There'll be trouble if she kills herself while I'm arresting her.'

'Don't do anything stupid!' he cried.

'I refuse to go back to a common prisoner's cell, Señor. Better for a Pulido to die than to agree to that. So if you don't want me dead, you'll wait while I take your horse and go.'

With that she ran – knife in hand – from the room, hurried from the house, jumped on the sergeant's horse, and rode off into the night.

'After her!' shouted Gonzales from the veranda.

pile a number of things one on top of the other

READING CHECK

Match the first and second parts of these sentences.

a Don Diego visits the governor

b Twenty-nine young men follow Zorro

c Zorro's men rescue the Pulidos from prison

d Zorro's men take Don Carlos

e Gonzales rides after Zorro

f Zorro hides Señorita Lolita

g Zorro rides away to hide

h Gonzales finds Lolita

1 but Don Carlos wants to stay there.

2 and Doña Catalina different ways.

3 but Don Diego says that he's ill and going to bed.

4 who tells him that the Pulidos are traitors.

5 in Fray Felipe's house.

6 in a native's small house by the highway.

7 but she escapes on his horse.

8 but he can't catch the outlaw.

WORD WORK

1 Use the picture clues to complete the sentences with new words from Chapter 7.

a There's a ....guard.... outside the building.

b She's lived in a small prison .... for many years.

c Do you think that a .... killed our chickens?

d They came to .... him at the hotel.

e There's a .... of books on my desk.

f He likes to write in a .... at the bottom of his garden.

2 **Find other words from Chapter 7 in the word-bit puzzle to complete the sentences below.**

r e	c u	u r h o	o n
c o	m m	g e d	s
e n	g h b o	t u	o d
r e s	d i v	e	t o
n e i	g a	i d e	r n

a She comes from a good family but her boyfriend is very ..common... .

b We live in a nice.................. . Everyone around us is very friendly.

c They can't................. home now because they have no home to go back to.

d At the end of the film, Superman................. Lois Lane from death.

e William is..................... .... Kate, and they're going to marry next year.

f When you................. six by two, you get three.

GUESS WHAT

Match the first and second parts of the sentences to find out what happens in the next chapter.

a Captain Ramón   **1** marries Señorita Lolita.

b Don Diego   **2** dies in a sword fight.

c The governor   **3** takes off his mask and shows his true face.

d Don Alejandro   **4** agrees that the Pulidos and Zorro can go free.

e Zorro   **5** tells the governor to leave south California.

Chapter 8 Behind the mask

After the soldiers rode past, Zorro left the native's hut. Then he jumped on his horse, and rode to the fort in Reina de Los Angeles. All the soldiers were away, looking for him. Only Captain Ramón sat in his office, waiting for news.

'You!' cried Ramón when the outlaw walked into his office, gun in hand.

'Stand with your hands behind your back!' came the reply. Zorro **tied** the captain's hands together.

'Where's the governor?' he asked.

'At Don Juan Estado's house,' answered Ramón.

'Then we'll visit him. And remember, my gun's at your head, so no noise.'

Outside the fort, Zorro told the captain to get on his horse. Then he himself got up behind, and they rode quietly over to Don Juan's house.

They went in through the back, and Zorro pushed the captain into the front room, following quickly. His Excellency and Don Juan were at a table, talking.

'Don't move,' said the outlaw.

'Zorro!' cried the governor. 'Why are you here?'

'To explain,' Zorro said. 'Excellency, today you wrongly put a gentleman's family in a common prison cell.'

'But they're traitors who've helped *you* – an outlaw!' came the governor's angry reply.

'Who told you that?'

'Captain Ramón. You had dinner at the Pulidos' country house. A native brought the news to the captain, who went after you. Don Carlos hid you in a closet, and when you came out, you **wounded** Ramón from behind with your sword and escaped.'

tie to keep something in place with string or rope

wound to hurt badly

48

'Captain, now tell the governor the true story. Don Carlos himself sent the native to the fort. The Pulidos didn't know that I was in the closet. And I gave you time to take out your sword and fight like a man, didn't I? Answer!'

'Yes. You're right,' said the captain.

'Is there anything more against the Pulidos, Excellency?'

'Yes. While Don Diego Vega was away, and the Pulidos were staying at his house, the captain visited one night, and found you there with the señorita. You're the Pulidos' friend, and they hid and helped you, even in the house of someone who's **loyal** to me. That night you escaped because the señorita stopped the captain catching you.'

loyal a person who is loyal does not change his friends

lie to say something that is not true; when you say something that is not true

hang to kill somebody by putting a rope round their neck and holding them above the ground

'Now for the true story,' said Zorro. 'Captain Ramón, you're in love with Señorita Lolita. You found her alone that night and tried to kiss her. She called for help. And I came and kicked you out of the house, didn't I? Speak!'

'Yes. That's right.'

'Captain Ramón, you've **lied** to me,' said the governor, 'You're no longer an officer.' Then he told the outlaw, 'But I'm still sure that the Pulidos are traitors. So my men will take them back to prison, and then I'll **hang** you.'

'We'll see,' replied Zorro, 'But I have something more to do before leaving, so you and Don Juan must sit over there.'

The governor and Don Juan sat by the window while Zorro told Ramón, 'You offended Señorita Lolita, and must pay for that. Your shoulder's better, and you have a sword, so fight me!'

Ramón's eyes were wild. The governor knew all about his lies, and so he was no longer a captain. He looked at Zorro darkly. He would kill this outlaw. Then perhaps His Excellency would **pardon** him.

He went over to the governor, saying, 'Untie me, Excellency, and I'll kill him.'

'Do that, and you can be a captain again,' said the governor, untying him at once.

Then the fight began. Ramón ran at his enemy, sword in hand, but Zorro fought back cleverly – his gun in his left hand, his sword in his right.

'Kill him, Ramón!' cried the governor. He and Don Juan knew that Zorro would shoot if they moved, so they sat still. Then Zorro threw his gun on the table.

'I'll use my sword, Excellency, if either of you tries anything,' he told the governor. But neither he nor Don Juan wanted to try.

Now Zorro's left hand was free, and he pushed Ramón back. The captain fought more weakly than before.

Suddenly Ramón **thrust** his sword wildly at Zorro, who jumped back unhurt. At once the outlaw's sword made three quick cuts on his enemy's face, leaving a red letter Z there. Then Zorro thrust his sword through Ramón's body, and the captain fell to the floor, dead.

'Now I'll leave,' said the outlaw.

'I'll hang you for this!' cried the governor.

'If you catch me!' laughed Zorro. He took his gun, ran outside, and jumped on his horse – ready to ride away.

But it was now early morning. Three groups of soldiers were

pardon to decide not to punish someone for a crime; when someone decides not to punish someone for a crime

thrust to push strongly and quickly

arriving back from Pala, the Pulidos' country house, and San Gabriel. And Zorro was in the middle of them.

Suddenly one of Gonzales's men saw him, crying, 'The Curse of Capistrano!' Zorro galloped across the square.

Just then, the governor and Don Juan ran into the street. 'Stop him! Murderer!' they cried.

He rode hard for the highway now, dividing the crowd of soldiers in his way.

'After him!' shouted Sergeant Gonzales angrily.

Then Zorro turned a corner in the road. But what was this? Someone was galloping into town, and behind them, a group of soldiers followed.

Which way now? Back, or straight on? He turned around but then, over his shoulder, he saw that the rider coming nearer was Señorita Lolita. 'Wait!' she cried. Soon she was by his side, and together they rode into town.

'I escaped from Fray Felipe's house,' began Lolita.

'Tell me later,' cried Zorro.

Suddenly there were soldiers with guns before them.

'Take them, dead or alive!' screamed Gonzales.

'Quickly! Do what I do!' called Zorro. He rode his horse fast at the men, jumping over them at the last minute.

Lolita followed. 'Where now?' she cried.

'To the tavern!'

They jumped off their horses and sent everyone out of the tavern before they locked the door.

In no time the square was full of soldiers. The governor arrived, and Sergeant Gonzales. Even Don Alejandro was there, with other gentleman of the neighbourhood.

'Everybody's here!' laughed Zorro, watching through a hole in the tavern door.

'Your young followers, too?' asked Lolita.

'No. For them it was only an exciting night adventure. Speaking out by day against the governor is harder. This is the end. I'm going to die.'

'*We're* going to die!' said Lolita. 'I can't live without you.'

Just then, a group of young gentlemen on horses arrived in the square and rode over to the governor.

'Stop!' shouted one.

'What's that?' cried the governor.

'We speak for all the gentlemen's families here. It was wrong to send the Pulidos to prison. You must pardon them. Zorro too must have a pardon. His only crimes are fighting against false justice and helping the weak and the poor.'

'What do you say, Don Alejandro Vega? Must I pardon these traitors and this outlaw?'

'You must,' answered Don Alejandro. 'I'm fully behind these gentlemen. Go back to San Francisco de Asis and leave south California to us. If you change your ways, we'll be loyal.'

'Very well,' said the governor. 'Then I pardon the Pulido family, and Señor Zorro, too!'

Everybody cheered, and Zorro and Lolita left the tavern, and walked into the square.

'So who are you?' cried Sergeant Gonzales. 'Show your face!'

Zorro took off his mask and everyone saw that he was – Don Diego! Everybody was terribly surprised.

Don Alejandro cried happily, 'My son! But how?'

'It began when I was fifteen,' explained Don Diego. 'I felt angry when the governor's men hurt the weak and poor in Capistrano, and I decided to fight back. I taught myself to use a sword and ride. I started wearing a mask, and called myself Zorro.

'It wasn't easy being Don Diego by day and Zorro by night, but none of you learned my secret. Not even Señorita Lolita, who refused to love Don Diego for his money, but loved Señor Zorro for his true heart! Now I'll marry her if she wants me, and then the governor will think twice before he makes enemies of the Pulidos again. My days as Zorro are over, but from now on I'll be a more manly Don Diego.

'And for you, friend Gonzales, the news that you gave Don Diego of where you were riding was most helpful to Zorro. I'm sorry that you won't have your reward, but I'll pay for drinks at the tavern for you and your men!'

'What a gentleman!' cried Sergeant Gonzales.

READING CHECK

Correct these false sentences.

a ~~Fray Felipe~~ Zorro takes Captain Ramón to the governor to explain things.

b The governor still thinks that the Vega family are traitors.

c Zorro fights with Gonzales and kills him.

d Zorro meets Señorita Lolita coming into town on the governor's horse.

e Together they run into the church in the town square.

f A young gentleman tells the governor to pardon the Pulidos and Fray Felipe.

g Don Diego says that he agrees with them, and the governor listens to him.

h When Zorro takes off his mask, people see that he is really Don Carlos.

WORD WORK

Complete the students' quiz conversation with the words in the mask.

hang

loyal

pardons

thrusts

wounded

lied

ties

Student A: Who ......ties...... Ramón's hands together?

Student B: Zorro does. Why does the governor think that Zorro .... Ramón from behind?

Student C: Because Ramón .... to him. Where does Zorro kill the captain and how?

Student D: He .... his sword through him in Don Juan Estado's house. How does the governor plan to kill Zorro?

Student E: He plans to .... him. But what does he do in the end?

Student F: He .... Zorro and the Pulidos. When is the governor surprised by Don Diego and why?

Student G: When Zorro takes off his mask, because His Excellency thought that Don Diego was .... to him and a coward.

Project A US Characters

1 Read about California and Zorro, and complete the information table below.

The State of California is on the West Coast of the United States. Its nickname is 'The Golden State' because of the gold there. The state capital is Sacramento and its biggest city is Los Angeles. California was part of the Spanish Empire in the late 1700s and early 1800s. In 1821 it became part of Mexico, after that country won its independence from Spain. In 1850 California became the 31st State to join the United States.

Zorro is a well-known fictional character from California. He first appeared in 1919 in the story 'The Curse of Capistrano' by Johnston McCulley. Different actors have played Zorro in films and on TV, including Anthony Hopkins and Antonio Banderas in 1998 and 2005.

State and nickname	....
	'The .... State'
	because of ....
State capital and biggest city	.... (capital)
	Biggest city: ....
When joined the US	.... (...................... state)
Fictional character	....
First appeared	In .... in the story ....
	.... by ....
Location	....
History before that	– part of ....
	– part of ....
Actors playing the character	.... and ....
	(in .... and ....)

2 Complete the text about Georgia and Scarlett O'Hara with information from the table.

State and nickname	Georgia
	'The Peach State' (because of its great fruit farms)
State capital and biggest city	Atlanta (capital)
	Biggest city: Atlanta
When joined the US, and which state	In 1788 (4th state); (left Union in 1861 during the American Civil War; re-joined in 1870)
Fictional character	Scarlett O'Hara
First appeared	In 1936 in the book 'Gone with the Wind' by Margaret Mitchell
Location	the southeastern United States
History before that	– colony of Britain (1732–1788)
Actresses playing the character	Vivien Leigh (1939 film)
	Joanne Whaley (1990s TV series)

The State of .... is in the .... United States. Its nickname is
'.................................' because .... is the
state capital and its biggest city, too. .... was a colony of ....
from .... to .... In .... it became the
.... state to join .... (but it left the Union from ....
to ...., during the ....).
.... is a well-known fictional character from .... She first
appeared in .... in the book '.................' by .... Different
actresses have played .... in the theatre, on TV, and in films – including
.... in the 1939 film and .... in the 1990s TV series.

3 Research another fictional American character and their state. Write a short article about them like the ones in activities 1 and 2.

Jay Gatsby in 'The Great Gatsby' (North Dakota)

Dorothy Gale in 'The Wizard of Oz' (Kansas)

Tom Sawyer in 'The Adventures of Tom Sawyer' (Missouri)

Jo March in 'Little Women' (Massachusetts)

Project B *Character Back Stories*

A 'back story' tells what happened to a character before the story begins. We understand a character better if we know their back story.

1 Match each back story with a character from Zorro.

a When she was a little girl, she loved listening to stories of adventure at bedtime. In those days, her family was rich and she had her own horse. She loved riding because she felt free doing it. But when her family lost all its money, they took her horse and sold it.

b He was an only child. His father drank, hit his mother when he got angry, and always told lies. After his father died from drink, he joined the army and sent money home to his mother. When his mother died, he began drinking and running after women.

c She was a rich shopkeeper's daughter. Her father wanted her to marry into a good family and found her a young gentleman with not much money to marry. She wanted lots of children, but her husband lost interest after her first child came.

d His father died young. He had a cleverer, better-looking older brother, and they fought over everything. His mother always took his brother's side. When his brother (now a doctor) married, he stole some money and ran away to become an army officer.

e He was the youngest of a big country family. His brothers liked working in the fields, but he wanted to read and write. His father laughed at this, but his mother took him to the village priest who taught him. After that, he decided to join the church.

f He came from a good family. He married for money, not for love, but over the years he has learned to love his wife. He really wanted a son, so when his daughter was born he decided to have no more children. Poor now, he is careful with his money.

Fray Felipe

Señorita Lolita

Doña Catalina

Captain Ramón

Don Carlos

Sergeant Gonzales

**2 Read these 'back story' sentences. Who do they belong to?
Mark them G (the governor) or A (Don Alejandro).**

a He never married, and has never run after women.

b He was always more interested in money than love.

c He married for love, and never stopped loving his wife.

d He was careful to say what the king wanted to hear.

e He never told lies, and he helped people weaker than him.

f He was never good with a sword, but he enjoyed punishing people.

g He preferred to have people around him who agreed with him.

h He decided to give important jobs to all his friends.

i His wife died when their son was still a young boy.

j He was never afraid when he was younger, and he fought well.

k He liked having expensive parties in San Francisco.

l He took money from his enemies to put in his pockets.

the Governor

Don Alejandro Vega

3 Make notes about Don Diego's back story in the table.

What stories did he like as a child?	
Who taught him to read and write?	
How did he feel when his mother died?	
What was his father like when he was a boy?	
What happened in Capistrano when he was 15?	
What did he decide to do about it?	
How did he learn to use a sword and ride?	
Who helped him to become Señor Zorro?	

4 Write Don Diego's back story, using your notes in activity 3 to help you.

GRAMMAR CHECK

Adverbs

We make adverbs from adjectives by adding –ly. For adjectives ending in –y, we change –y to –i and add –ly.

Add –ly	*quick*	*quickly*
Add –ily	*thirsty*	*thirstily*

We use adverbs to describe actions.

Sergeant Gonzales called for more wine thirstily. He got angry quickly.

1 Write the adverbs of these adjectives.

  a angry   ...*angrily*...

  b clever   ....

  c happy   ....

  d heavy   ....

  e loving   ....

  f secret   ....

  g silent   ....

  h sudden   ....

2 Complete the sentences using an adverb from exercise 3.

  a Gonzales answered the landlord ...*angrily*... when he began talking about Zorro.

  b ....the tavern door opened, and someone hurried in.

  c Don Diego never looked .... at women, never fought, nor drank much.

  d Gonzales drank ...., and always spoke of women and fighting.

  e Zorro fought Gonzales ...., his eyes like cold fire.

  f Everybody listened .... while Gonzales explained about the fight.

  g Don Diego turned to the fire and smiled ....

  h Don Carlos agreed .... when Don Diego asked to marry Lolita.

GRAMMAR CHECK

Yes/No questions and short answers

We use auxiliary verbs or the correct forms of be (main verb) in Yes/No questions.	In the short answers we re-use the auxiliary verb or the correct form of be.
Will you marry me?	*No, I won't.*
Must I court you?	*Yes, you must.*
Are you Zorro?	*Yes, I am.*

3 **Write Zorro's answers to Don Carlos's questions.**

a Have you come to steal from me?   .No, I haven't.

b Can I take my wife to her room?   ....

c Can I take my daughter with me?   ....

d Will you take off your mask for us?   ....

e Do they call you 'the Curse of Capistrano'?   ....

f Did you begin your outlaw's life in the town of Capistrano?   ....

g Do you cut the letter Z on your enemies' faces?   ....

h Have you met Sergeant Gonzales?   ....

i Will the governor give a reward to the man who kills you?   ....

j Would you like some food for the road?   ....

k Can you tell us one last story?   ....

l Did your horse gallop away with you on its back earlier?   ....

m Have you killed Captain Ramón?   ....

n Will the captain die?   ....

GRAMMAR

GRAMMAR CHECK

To + infinitive or –ing form verb

After the verbs *begin*, *enjoy*, *finish*, *go*, *like*, *love*, *remember*, and *stop*, we use verb + –ing.

Lolita remembered Zorro kissing her hand.

After the verbs *ask*, *begin*, *hope*, *like*, *need*, *try*, *want*, and *would* like, we use to + infinitive.

I'd like to invite you to my town house.

4 **Complete these sentences about the story with the to + infinitive or verb + –ing form of the verb in brackets.**

a Sergeant Gonzales goes ....*riding*.... (ride) into the hills after Zorro.

b Gonzales finishes .... (tell) lies about Zorro when he hears Ramón's story.

c Don Diego hopes .... (marry) Lolita.

d He needs .... (travel) to his country house.

e Lolita likes .... (visit) the town when she can.

f She enjoys .... (read) love poetry.

g She begins .... (think) differently when she sees Don Diego's books.

h Captain Ramón wants .... (kiss) Lolita.

i She tries .... (escape) from him.

j She stops .... (worry) when Zorro arrives.

k She loves .... (be) with the outlaw.

l She asks him .... (leave) his criminal life and marry her.

63

GRAMMAR

GRAMMAR CHECK

Past Simple and Past Continuous

We use the Past Simple to describe events in the past. Many Past Simple affirmative verbs end in –d (*escaped*), –ed (*stayed*), or –ied (*hurried*). There are also many irregular verbs (*sit – sat*; *write – wrote*).

Captain Ramón hurried to the fort. There he sat down and wrote to the governor.

We use the Past Continuous to talk about an activity that began before – and was in progress when – the events in the Past Simple occurred. To make it, we use was/were + the present participle.

When Zorro left Don Diego's house, his horse was waiting for him.
   Past Simple   Past Continuous

5 Answer the questions about the story. Use the words in brackets.

a What was Ramón doing while he read his copy of the letter?
(smile) .He..was..smiling..

b What did Zorro do after he left Don Diego's house? (ride/fort) ....

c What was Ramón doing when Zorro walked by his window?
(talk/himself) ....

d What were most of the soldiers from the fort doing? (look for/Zorro) ....

e What did Zorro do to the soldier at the fort door? (hit/head) ....

f What did Zorro do with the copy of the letter after he read it? (burn/it) ....

g What was Gonzales doing when Ramón shouted for help? (talk/his men) ....

6 Complete the text using the Past Simple or the Past Continuous.

While Don Diego **a)** .was..looking.. (look) out of the tavern door, he saw that two soldiers **b)** .... (ride) into town and that Fray Felipe **c)** .... (walk) between their horses, their prisoner. The landlord **d)** .... (tell) Don Diego what **e)** ....(happen). 'The priest **f)** .... (cheat) a merchant, and now he must go before the magistate,' he **g)** .... (explain). Don Diego **h)** .... (hurry) across to the magistrate's office. When the soldiers **i)** .... (arrive) with Fray Felipe, Don Diego **j)** .... (speak) with the magistrate. The merchant and his son **k)** .... (stand) on the other side of the room, ready to tell their story.

GRAMMAR CHECK

Information questions and question words

We use question words in information questions. We answer these questions by giving some information.

What's the name of Zorro's horse? I don't know.

Why does Captain Ramón hate Zorro? Because he's bad and Zorro's good.

How many children does Don Carlos have? Only one – Señorita Lolita.

7 **Complete the information questions with the question words in the box.**

> how   how many   how much   what   when
> where   which   ~~who~~   who   why

a Q: ......Who...... is Don Diego Vega's father?

A: Don Alejandro.

b Q: .... has Don Diego decided to marry?

A: Señorita Lolita.

c Q: .... has Lolita refused to marry Diego?

A: Because he didn't court her.

d Q: .... more time does Don Alejandro give his son to find a wife?

A: Three months.

e Q: .... will Don Alejandro do if Diego hasn't married by that time?

A: Leave all his money to the church when he dies.

f Q: .... young gentlemen visit Don Alejandro's house?

A: Ten.

g Q: .... does Don Diego go just before Zorro arrives?

A: To his room.

h Q: .... does Don Alejandro feel because his son is asleep during Zorro's visit?

A: Terrible.

i Q: .... does Don Diego come out of his room?

A: After Zorro has left.

j Q: .... suit does Don Diego wear to go and court Lolita?

A: His finest one.

GRAMMAR CHECK

Reported speech with *said (that)*

We can use said (that) to introduce reported speech.

In direct speech sentences we give the exact words that people say.	We put reported speech verbs one step into past and change personal pronouns, possessive adjectives, and time expressions.
'I'm happy to see you today!' said His Excellency to Don Diego.	*His Excellency said (that) he was happy to see Don Diego that day.*
'I'll wait here for them to bring Zorro to me,' he said.	*He said (that) he would wait there for them to bring Zorro to him.*

8 Rewrite these direct speech sentences in reported speech.

a 'Other gentlemen won't think it right to put the Pulidos in prison,' said Don Diego.

Don Diego said (that) other gentlemen wouldn't think it right to put the Pulidos in prison.

b 'If they're under house arrest, Zorro will rescue them,' said the governor.

....

c 'I'm sure that Zorro will rescue the Pulidos this evening,' said young Vega's friend.

....

d 'I'm starting to feel ill just thinking of it,' said Don Diego.

....

e 'Don Diego's in bed and is seeing nobody,' said one of the young gentlemen.

....

f 'There's a reward for the man who catches Zorro,' said Sergeant Gonzales.

....

g 'The governor will punish us if we don't take the outlaw tonight,' said Gonzales.

....

h 'We're looking for something of Zorro's at your house,' said the sergeant to the priest.

....

i 'I don't know what you mean,' said Fray Felipe to Gonzales.

....

j 'I refuse to go back to a common prison cell,' said Lolita Pulido.

....

GRAMMAR

GRAMMAR CHECK

Question tags

We can use question tags to check information, or to ask someone to agree with us.

The tag contains subject + main verb or auxiliary verb to match the sentence.

When the sentence is affirmative, the tag is negative.

Don Carlos sent the native to the fort, didn't he?

When the sentence is negative, the tag is affirmative.

The Pulidos didn't know I was in the closet, did they?

We do not repeat the name in a question tag, we use a pronoun instead.

9 Complete the sentences with the question tags from the box.

are they   aren't you   did he   did I   did she   didn't I
didn't she   didn't you   wasn't she   ~~have they~~   haven't they

a The Pulidos haven't helped me, ...*have they*..?

b I gave you time to fight like a man, ...?

c I didn't wound you from behind, ...?

d Don Carlos didn't hide me in the closet, ...?

e The Pulidos aren't traitors, ...?

f You're in love with Señorita Lolita, ...?

g She was alone when you walked in, ...?

h You tried to kiss her, ...?

i She called for help, ...?

j She didn't help me to escape, ...?

k The Pulidos have been loyal to the governor, ...?

DOMINOES — THE STRUCTURED APPROACH TO READING IN ENGLISH

Dominoes is an enjoyable series of illustrated classic and modern stories in four carefully graded language stages – from Starter to Three – which take learners from beginner to intermediate level.

Each *Domino* reader includes:

- **a good story** to read and enjoy
- **integrated activities** to develop reading skills and increase active vocabulary
- **personalized projects** to make the language and story themes more meaningful
- **seven pages of grammar activities** for consolidation.

Each *Domino* pack contains a reader, plus a MultiROM with:

- **a complete audio recording of the story**, fully dramatized to bring it to life
- **interactive activities** to offer further practice in reading and language skills and to consolidate learning.

If you liked this Level Two *Domino*, why not read these?

The Bird of Happiness and Other Wise Tales
Tim Herdon

What is the secret of happiness, or the best thing for a wife to take with her when she leaves home?

How does a man pay for the smell of bread, or decide if he is lucky?

What happens when a friend steals a gift meant for you, or is careless when he tries to make his dreams of a better life come true?

How can you change dirt into gold, or get what you want?

The eight wise tales in this collection teach us some important lessons about life.

Book ISBN: 978 0 19 424919 5
MultiROM Pack ISBN: 978 0 19 424917 1

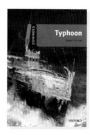

Typhoon
Joseph Conrad

'There's some bad weather out there,' Captain MacWhirr said to himself just before he sailed his ship, the *Nan-Shan*, into the middle of the most terrible storm in the South China Sea.

The typhoon brings out the best in some men on the ship, and the worst in others.

Can MacWhirr bring the ship through the storm safely? And what will happen to all the poor Chinese workers travelling home down in the ship's hold?

Book ISBN: 978 0 19 424893 8
MultiROM Pack ISBN: 978 0 19 424845 7

You can find details and a full list of books in the *Dominoes* catalogue and Oxford English Language Teaching Catalogue, and on the website: www.oup.com/elt

Teachers: see www.oup.com/elt for a full range of online support, or consult your local office.

	CEFR	Cambridge Exams	IELTS	TOEFL iBT	TOEIC
Level 3	B1	PET	4.0	57-86	550
Level 2	A2–B1	KET-PET	3.0-4.0	–	–
Level 1	A1–A2	YLE Flyers/KET	3.0	–	–
Starter & Quick Starter	A1	YLE Movers	–	–	–